Never Quite Ours

Meghan White

Contents

Chapter 1

COLD SPRING AIR creeps in through the gap between the windows, and outside, the sun has only just begun to set. But time seems to have stopped for her, because her world has shifted off its axis.

It starts with the shrill ring of the phone, and then a voice choked with desperation. "Emma, there's been an accident," the person on the other end of the line says. "It's Dylan, he's—"

She doesn't hear anything more after that. It's as though an invisible force has sucker-punched her right in the gut, and dragged the oxygen out of her lungs. She pulls in a deep breath for air that refuses to come, and squeezes her eyes shut. There's a roaring in her ears, louder than anything she's ever heard before, and all she can think is: please not him, not him, not him, nothim, nothim nothim nothim...

Somewhere in the back of her mind, she registers that the jumbled words sound a lot like 'nothing'.

It's seconds, maybe minutes—but it feels like an eternity, before she pulls herself together. Her phone flashes with a new text from Dylan's sister, Morgan, with the address of the hospital and his room number. Her hands and feet move on autopilot. Grab her bag, shoes, jacket, phone, car keys. Shut the door. Down the elevator; into the car. Key in the ignition; check the rearview mirror.

It's all these little things that keep her afloat while her mind feels like it's drowning. With only the headlights to guide her, she feels a lot like a sailor lost at sea with a lighthouse as her sole lifeline. But how can a light save a sailor, if the waves are already too big?

By the time she arrives at the hospital, the sun has already set. She rushes towards room 602, and stops when she sees a small group of people gathered in the hallway. His parents are there, his little sister, as well as several nurses. There's even a policeman or two—she recognises them by their uniforms. Her heart pounds wildly in her chest as she struggles to catch her breath.

"How is he?" she manages to ask.

His family immediately turns, and while his dad only gives her a watery smile, his mum rushes up to her. "Emma, I'm so sorry," the older woman says, as she pulls Emma into a tight hug.

Emma's heart drops. "Is he—?"

"No, he's not!" Morgan rolls her eyes and lets out an exasperated sigh. "Damn it, Mum, don't scare her like that!"

"But he hasn't woken up yet, and the doctors say that he's very badly injured," his dad explains. Despite his calm voice, Emma can sense a hint of urgency and knows he's just as worried as they all are. He pulls Dylan's mum aside and wraps an arm around her. "We're all hoping for the best."

Emma nods and moves closer to where they are. Taking a deep breath, she looks into the room. She could prepare herself a dozen times for this, but nothing will ever be enough for this moment.

He looks...broken.

That's the only word she can think of. Bandages and tubes are wrapped around him, like a maze he can't get out of. Her breath catches in her throat. He's so bruised and pale, that he seems almost lifeless.

Wake up, she thinks, as she presses a palm against the window. Once, he used to joke about how they knew each other so well that they might as well be telepathic. She'd just laughed it off then, but she hopes desperately that it's true now. She wonders if they can do it. Please wake up.

"Are you the patient's girlfriend?" She turns at the unfamiliar voice, only to find one of the policemen headed towards her. When she nods, the man continues, "Do you have any idea where Mr Torres was driving to?"

"He was headed home, I think," she says quietly. "He texted that he had to work overtime, and that we'd go out later for dinner."

"Is this your address?" The cop holds out a slip of paper, with her address scrawled across it. She nods, surprised, and he points to Dylan's parents, who've been taken aside by the doctors. "We asked them for your address to check his destination. Based on the route he was taking, though, it seems like he wasn't headed towards your home."

"What?"

"He was driving in the opposite direction." The cop places a sealed bag into her arms. "Here are the things he had on him when the paramedics pulled him out of the wreck. These are all his, correct?"

One quick glance and she nods. They're all Dylan's. His phone, his jacket, his wallet. Their keys. To their home. That he apparently wasn't driving to.

"One more thing," says the policeman. "Do you know what this is?"

He holds up another slip of paper, barely the size of a post-it note. And in brisk, sharp handwriting are the words:

Told you you'd regret it.

Chapter 2

"CAN I COME in?"

At the sound of the familiar voice, she glances over to the doorway. He's leaning against the doorframe, with a small smile that seems to brighten the whole place. She returns his smile, then tries not to wince as the cut on her lip begins to sting. "Sure."

"I'm not bothering you, am I?" he asks, as he saunters over with that usual confidence he has. But she's spent enough time watching him to notice the little things: the way he falters as he reaches her bed, his hand fiddling with the strap of his bag, and the other hidden behind his back.

"Not at all," she assures him. "My friend just left, and I've no visitors for the rest of the afternoon."

"Your friend?" He throws a glance over his shoulder, then turns back to her. "Is that the girl who just left? She looked pretty upset."

"Yeah, that's Scout. She's on her way to break up with her boyfriend. She doesn't trust him very much after...this whole thing," Emma explains, waving a vague hand around the room. "She seems to think that he's a little responsible for what happened. I told her that there's no solid proof he knew, but she's pretty adamant about it so..."

"He probably knew," Dylan says unexpectedly.

"Really?"

"Yeah." He shifts a little on his feet and continues, "I heard that they were good friends, and they hung out all the time, so it's likely that he was at least a little aware of it."

She lets out a slow breath. "It doesn't matter if he knew. It's not his fault anyway. It's no one else's fault but the one who put me here."

Dylan nods, but he doesn't say anything to that. His gaze meets hers, honest and open, and heat rises to her cheeks. She quickly lowers her eyes and gestures to the chair beside her bed. "Have a seat."

He starts to sit, then stops. "I brought you something. Two things, actually." He finally raises his other hand that he's kept hidden behind his back, and holds out a single, long-stemmed white daisy.

A small smile flits across her face as she takes the daisy from him. "You bought this for me?"

"Yeah." He averts his gaze from hers and reaches into his bag. "And one more thing."

For a moment or two, she stares in silent confusion at the golden trophy that he's holding out to her. And then she realises what it is. Her smile grows. "Your team won?"

"Just regionals," he says, with a shrug. "It's not a big deal."

"It is a big deal, I've seen how hard you train the team. Congratulations, I knew you could do it." She admires the shiny trophy for awhile, before a thought occurs to her. "The match was today?"

"Yes."

"Then what're you doing here, instead of being at the after-game party?"

He clears his throat and shrugs again. "It's always the same thing. Same people, same parties. And I wanted to see you," he adds, as he settles down on the chair beside her bed. From the pink on his cheeks, it's clear that he's a little embarrassed by his bold admission, but he forges on anyway and fixes her with a steady gaze.

Oh, she knows that look. She's not blind or oblivious, after all. It's a look that cuts right to her heart; she can feel a slight, involuntary ripple that spreads through her, warm and lovely. But she fists her hands within the blanket and steels herself.

"Listen, Emma," he says, "there's something I've been meaning to tell you—"

"Dylan, before you say anything..." she trails off and takes a deep breath. "I'm leaving."

"What?"

"I spoke with my dad last night," she says quietly, looking down at her lap. "The school told my parents what happened and they're not happy. Dad's already preparing his team of lawyers, and he and mum will fly over first thing this weekend. But they want me to go back with them, and they want me to attend another school. That used to be my dream school before we moved here, and it obviously has much better prospects, but..."

"You should go."

She looks up. "Really?"

He meets her gaze steadily and nods. And when he smiles at her, it's genuine, even if a bit sad. "I've told you this before, Emma, you're way too smart to be stuck in this old town. You should grab any opportunity you can with both hands, and never let go. It's your dream, after all, and you shouldn't have to give it up again."

Something tightens in her chest. It's not sadness; it's not hurt. She rarely ever feels any of those emotions around him. It's gratitude—that finally, someone understands her so perfectly; and a hint of wistfulness—the what-we-could-have-been-but-will-never-be that hangs in the air between them.

"Thank you," she tells him softly.

He smiles and shakes his head. "When do you leave?"

"Probably by the end of this summer."

"That's not too bad. And, hey, who knows? Maybe we'll still get to meet each other in the future."

The corners of her lips finally lift in response to his infectious smile. "I'd like that," she says. She doesn't hope for many things, but, this time, she hopes desperately that she'll get to see him again.

Chapter 3

- -

"**I**S THIS SEAT taken?"

"No, go ahead," she says, without glancing away from the sign-up sheet. There are only ten spots left to meet her professor during office hours, and it's of utmost importance that she gets it. She scribbles her name on the form and finally looks up.

She blinks.

"Oh, hey." The boy standing in front of her looks just as surprised as she feels. He grins and dumps his bag on their table, then settles down on the chair beside hers. "I thought you looked familiar. This is table E, right?"

She stares at the popsicle stick in his hand that has the letter 'E' written on it. And then at her own stick that she'd picked up from the front desk earlier, which also has the same letter.

Huh. Seems like they're really lab partners, then.

"What're you doing here?" she asks, still confused. "This is a freshman class."

"No, this is a class that freshmen can take, not a class for freshmen. It's one of my required electives." His eyes twinkle as he lowers his voice and continues, "I'll let you in on a little secret. When it comes to classes like these that are open to anyone, priority is usually given to the students who need to graduate. The more you delay taking it, the more advantageous it becomes for you, because you have the experience and knowledge over all these freshmen, while the professor still grades at a freshmen level. See that guy over there? He's a senior taking all the freshmen level classes this semester while he works on his final thesis."

She scrunches her nose a little. "That doesn't seem very fair."

"It's not," he says, with an unrepentant grin. "Just last year, I had to deal with elitist seniors who wrecked the bell curve, and now I'm the sophomore who'll wreck the bell curve. It's a vicious cycle, but it's the end result that matters, right? To graduate with first-class honours?"

She falls silent at that, because he's not entirely wrong. Even if this is a terribly unfair workaround, she'd be a hypocrite to pretend like it wouldn't be nice to have the edge over other people. And her grades really are that important.

His smile widens when she doesn't say anything. "You're already filing this away for future use, aren't you?"

Damn him. She bites her lip and looks away.

He chuckles and starts to take out his laptop from his bag. "So you really followed your boyfriend here?"

"Yes, he really wants to make the football team."

"Football, huh? What's his name?"

"Keith Jacobs."

"Keith Jacobs..." He frowns for a moment or two, before he nods. "Yeah, I think I remember him. He was at tryouts last week."

She brightens at that. "He's very good, isn't he?" she presses, eagerly. "Do you think he'll make it in?"

He starts to respond, but then stops, his eyes narrowing. "Are you trying to influence my decisions because you know that I'm the football captain?"

"No, I'm simply reminding you how talented he is, because I know that you, as the valedictorian before me, are smart enough to make the right decision."

He blinks at her, clearly taken aback by her response, before he breaks out into a laugh. His laugh is so genuine and sudden that it attracts the attention of the other students around them, but he doesn't seem to care. He shakes his head in mirth; his hair falling into his eyes. "Well played—" he pauses, and leans forward to read her name from the sign-up sheet. "—Emma Chen. Really well played."

"Thank you—" she starts to say his name, but for the life of her, she can't recall what it is. She makes a mental note, there and then, to remember his name.

Chapter 4

SHE STIRS AWAKE at the sound of someone calling her name. At first, a surge of hope rises within her and she thinks that it's Dylan calling her. But—no, the voice is decidedly feminine, and when she lifts her head, it's Dylan's mom who's peering down at her in concern.

"Emma, honey," she says in a soft voice. "Why don't you and Morgan get some sleep in the waiting room? Dylan's dad and I will keep him company."

She straightens and looks around the room. It's been a long day, and his family looks just as tired as she feels. In between talking to the doctors and helping with police investigations, it seems that none of them has gotten any proper rest.

So far, it's a dead end: there are no traffic cameras along that part of the road, nor can the police identify where the note came from. They aren't ruling out the possibility that the note could be entirely unrelated to the accident either.

That just makes Emma all the more unsettled and reluctant to leave his side. "No, thank you," she tells his mom. "I'm not going anywhere until he wakes up."

"There's no telling when he'll wake up," Morgan points out. "The doctors say it could be anytime between minutes to days, and he really does like to sleep. Once, during summer break, he even slept for three days straight."

"Morgan." Mrs Torres shakes her head reprovingly, before offering Emma a small smile. "He'll wake up. I'm just worried that you'll fall sick by the time he does, and then he'll never let us hear the end of it for not taking good care of you."

"She's right," Mr Torres says. "At least take a walk for a bit. Stretch your legs. Don't stay holed up in here."

She looks down at Dylan for a long moment. His face, usually tanned but pale now, and matted hair. Her fingers twitch by her sides, yearning to brush his hair out of his eyes. Why didn't she do that earlier?

He's lying so terribly still that she wonders if he's even breathing. Even before, she'd pressed her palm to his heart just to make sure she could still feel him.

Wake up, she wills him. Please wake up.

But he doesn't, and she's left with the bitter tang of disappointment once again. "Okay," she says quietly. "I'll go get something to eat."

"Take Morgan with you," says Dylan's dad. "Someone needs to keep an eye on our resident troublemaker."

Morgan makes a face and grumbles under her breath, but Emma knows what he really means: he wants Morgan to make sure she's okay. She offers Dylan's parents a faint smile and gets up, heading for the door with Morgan.

A faint rustle stops her in her tracks. Then Mrs Torres's voice, with a slight edge to it—"Dylan, honey? Frank, he's waking up, get the nurse just in case."

Emma whirls around; her heart in her throat. He's awake. She rushes back to his side; a brilliant smile spreading across her face. She can't remember the last time she felt this relieved.

"Hey," she breathes.

He blinks, once or twice, and gazes around the room with a slightly dazed look on his face. His eyes finally latch onto someone—but it's not her. "Hey, monkey," he rasps at last.

Morgan smirks and settles down on the edge of his bed. "Hey yourself. You scared the hell out of us, you know?"

His lips twitch up in a fraction of a smile, before his gaze lands on Emma. He blinks, then turns to the other side where his mum is. "Hi, mum."

"Dylan, thank God," his mum says, patting his cheek. "We were so worried when the hospital called."

"What—what happened?"

"Car accident," Morgan says briskly. "Police are still investigating."

His eyes widen. "Did I hit someone?"

Emma almost smiles at that. It's just like him to worry that he was the culprit instead of the victim. But before Morgan can reply, his dad comes bustling into the room. "Doctor is on her way," he says, stopping by the other side of Dylan's bed. "How're you feeling, son?"

"Not too good," Dylan admits, with a cough. Emma quickly pours him a glass of water and holds it to his lips. After a cursory glance her way, he reaches for it and takes a small sip.

She frowns. Something is wrong.

"As long as you're awake," his dad continues. "Emma was really worried about you, you know? She hasn't left your side all day."

Dylan stares at his parents, then at his sister standing by the foot of his bed. He hands Emma back the glass with a polite nod, the way a patient would to a nurse, and that's when she realizes that something is very, very wrong. And, with a sinking sense of dread, she knows full well the words that will leave his mouth as soon as he says them.

"Who's Emma?"

Chapter 5

THE POT OF shasta daisies on the windowsill has started to wilt. In all the chaos over the past few days, she's forgotten to water it. Dylan had bought it for her as part of his 'housewarming gifts' when they moved in together, and it's one of the things she loves most in this house.

It's one of the things she loves most in their little house. It reminds her of late spring, dew on the grass and baby blue skies. But most of all, it reminds her of them: she, the pot of daisies, always looking out for him, the sun, to bloom and grow.

But now, there's a small, vindictive part of her that wants to let it wilt away. Why should she care for it when he's forgotten all about her? She stares at the daisies for a long moment, before she gives in with a sigh and waters it anyway.

As she wanders down the empty hallway back to the living room, she finds that every little thing reminds her of him. He's in all of their photos on the mantelpiece above the fireplace; he's in the polaroids she's hung up on the wall. There's a ring of coffee stains on the table where he usually leaves his mug; the post-its he leaves her are scattered everywhere; Google home still recognizes his voice.

This house is him. It's her. It's them. He's like ivy that grows along the walls, entrenched so deeply that his mark is everywhere, and if he were to be removed, things will no longer be the same. She will never be the same.

"Emma." The voice breaks her out of her thoughts. She looks up, only to find her best friend staring at her in clear concern. Scout frowns a little and pushes the box aside. "You okay?"

Briefly, Emma considers lying, but she knows that her friend will see through her anyway. "No," she admits with a sigh, and wanders over to settle down amidst the pile of boxes. "I'm just...really sad, that's all. He remembers everyone but me, and I don't know why."

"That's not true," Scout points out gently. "It's not just you he doesn't remember. It's also everything that's happened in recent years—his job, his newer friends, even his years in college. Wasn't that what the doctors said? Something about post..."

"Post-traumatic amnesia," Emma recites—she can practically say this in her sleep now. "Or retrograde amnesia. He's suffering from a brain injury, and he just can't remember."

Doesn't want to remember, a little voice adds in her head. The look on his face when his family had told him who she was had been nothing but confused. Then frustrated. And then downright hostile, especially when Morgan kept calling him an idiot and a liar for not remembering who Emma was.

It really wasn't his fault. Half his mind was like a slate wiped clean. It just so happened that that part of the slate was her. But he didn't know that, and so he'd gotten so worked up that he'd upset the drip attached to his arm. She'd immediately left then, after giving her statement to the police and politely excusing herself to his worried parents. She'd promised to come back another day.

It's another day now, and she still hasn't summoned the courage to go back. According to his parents, Dylan is still volatile and suspicious whenever her name is mentioned. Morgan being Morgan doesn't help matters either. And Emma would much rather Dylan treat her with the polite indifference of a stranger, than the cruel hostility reserved for someone he hates.

"This is so wild," Scout remarks, shaking her head. "Retrograde amnesia is a trope straight out of every cliché novel."

Emma's lips twist in a bitter smile. "Except this novel is now my life, and it's kind of awful."

Scout offers her a sympathetic smile and pulls her into a brief hug. "If you're rock bottom now, you can only go up from here," she says softly, before she pulls away. "So, what's the plan?"

"What?"

"The plan. You always have a plan, even when things are at their worst. I'm sure you've already thought of something to fix this situation."

Emma's face brightens a little at that—Scout really does know her. "I do, actually. That's why we're going through all this stuff," she explains, gesturing to the boxes around them. "I mean, yes, I have to put together a few things in an overnight bag for his parents to bring to the hospital. But I'm also looking for...reminders."

"Reminders?"

"Just little things that might seem insignificant to anyone else, but were once important in our relationship." She points to the small pile of things she's set aside. "Like that chemistry textbook from the class we took together in college. Or that gift card from the first time we met, and I kept it as a memento instead of using it. I hope that whenever he sees these things, he'll know that they're from me. So that even if he can't remember me, he'll know that I'm still here."

"What about this?" Scout straightens out a crumpled piece of paper and begins reading off it. "Eggs, milk, chicken, ramen... Is this from the first time you guys went grocery shopping together?"

Emma's lips twitch. "No, that's just from last week's grocery shopping."

"Whoops." Scout crumples the paper back up and tosses it into the wastepaper bin across the room. It falls in with a silent swoosh, and Emma breaks into a small smile. Not for the first time, she marvels at how the down-to-earth, a little tomboyish, rough around the edges girl she'd befriended in college has matured to become the wise and caring woman she knows now, with a husband and a baby, and a knack for basketball tricks using the most ordinary things.

Scout's come a long way since college, but then, so has she.

"I can't believe you still have this!" Scout says, as she pulls out a stack of Denver high school yearbooks. "I've not seen these in forever—Dave doesn't keep anything from our high school days because he doesn't have many good memories from then. He says I was his only good memory."

"That's really sweet of him."

"You'd think, but then he said that vanilla cupcakes are his one true love, while he had our baby on his lap, so, you know. Pinch of salt and all that." Scout flips through a couple of pages, and then lets out a small sound of delight. "Oh, look! That's me!"

Emma immediately leans over to get a look. Seventeen-year old Scout has short brown hair, tons of freckles and looks plainly nervous in the picture. A few pages later, there's young Emma—with black hair framing wide eyes and a shy smile. Dylan is in the year above them, and his picture comes first as president of the senior year. Bright eyes, relaxed features and a confident smile.

There's something both nostalgic and strange about seeing old photos. She can barely recognize her young self, so different from the person she is now. It's almost like staring at a stranger—is this what Dylan sees when he looks at her now? Is this what it's like to forget? To have your memories distilled, dismantled and distorted through the passage of time, until you can no longer remember, with crystal clarity, what once was.

It's not quite the same as retrograde amnesia, of course, but suddenly, she feels a strong pang of sadness for him. He must be feeling so lost. And without her to guide him, he would be so alone.

She takes a deep breath and resolves to visit him as soon as she can. Her little reverie is broken when Scout lets out a small laugh beside her. "This is so weird," her best friend muses, now on a new page of the yearbook. "Dave in my mind looks exactly how he does now, but my ex doesn't. In my mind, he looks just like how he did at eighteen."

Emma stares at the picture that Scout's pointing to. Wild hair, dark eyes, and not a hint of a smile. "How did you know?" Scout asks. Emma glances at her in confusion, and she adds, "How did you know that Callum Wright would get into trouble from the very beginning?"

The difference between retrograde amnesia and the passage of time is this: the passage of time can be bridged in an instant. Sometimes, all it takes is a single word or two for the memories to come flooding back, with a crystalline clarity as though it happened just yesterday.

In this case, the words are Callum Wright.

"I had a hunch," Emma says softly.

Chapter 6

<hr style="border-top: 2px dashed;">

"Excuse me."

All around her is a blur of faces and voices as she pushes her way through the crowd. Finally, she manages to get some breathing room—a small space by the alcove beneath the stairs. In her little corner, she has a bird's eye view of Keith and his friends seated in the kitchen.

Just once—just once. She needs to get something on him. Anything.

True enough, barely a minute or so later, a group of guys head into the kitchen. There's a conversation exchanged that she can't hear, but she can see it perfectly. She reaches for her phone, ready to hit the record button, as one of Keith's friends dig into their bag and—

"Whoops, sorry!"

She nearly drops her phone when someone collides right into her. The girl is slightly tipsy, judging by the way she stumbles around on her feet, and she waves a hand right in Emma's face by way of apology.

"Sorry again, didn't mean to do that!" the girl says. Then she stops and peers closely at Emma. On instinct, Emma takes a quick step back, but the girl only flashes her a lopsided smile. "Oh, hey, you're Keith's girlfriend, right? Have you seen my boyfriend, Callum?"

Emma can't stop herself from glancing to the right. Keith is still there. So is this girl's boyfriend, Callum Wright. And, judging by their pleased looks, they've just secured themselves a very lucrative, but very illegal, deal.

"Oh, there he is!" the girl says as she follows Emma's gaze. Her smile widens and starts to head towards her boyfriend.

But, quick as thought, Emma grabs her by the hand. "You should leave."

The girl whirls around; her eyes wide. "What?"

"Get out while you still can." The words slip out of Emma's mouth before she can stop herself. "Because if you don't, you might never be able to leave."

The other girl starts to say something, but a movement in their peripheral catches Emma's eye. Callum Wright has started to look over towards them. Whether he can see them through the crowd or not is debatable, but Emma won't stay to find out.

She turns on her heels and quickly leaves, ignoring the girl when she calls after her. But she comes to a halt as she approaches the front door. Shite. A few guys from the football team are there too. If she tries to get past them, it's only a matter of time before Keith finds out that she came to the party. She immediately makes a u-turn and races up the stairs. She'll just have to hide in one of the rooms until it's safe to leave.

It's not until she opens one of the doors that she realizes what a horrible decision she's made.

Under any normal circumstances, she should've been able to hear them before the sooner the door. But the music downstairs is too loud, and the place is too dark here. It takes her a moment or two to realize what's going on. A quiet gasp escapes her, and she quickly shuts the door. But it's too late—she's already recognized one of the two people in the room.

Florence Ayrton.

Outside, Emma recoils from the door like it's a poisonous snake. Anyone would recognize the streak of rebellious red hair anywhere. She shivers and squeezes her eyes shut and—what the actual hell, that was not a sight she wanted to see. It's going to take awhile to burn that mental image out of her head. She pulls herself together and turns towards the stairs, only to stop dead in her tracks.

It's Dylan.

"Hey." The boy coming up the stairs grins at her, and his smile is so bright, so genuinely happy, that she takes a step back. "I thought you said you weren't coming."

She swallows hard. She's never been a very good liar. If she were, she wouldn't be stuck in a relationship that's lasted way past its expiration date. "I, um, wh-what're you doing here?"

His eyebrows go up. "This is my house? And that's my room," he adds, pointing to the door behind her. Her heart sinks even further. "I left my jacket in there and I need to get it, so..."

She sidesteps him when he reaches for the doorknob. "Why don't you head downstairs first, and I'll get it for you?"

"You want to go into my room?" There's a hint of amusement in his voice. "Do you even know where it is?"

"Sure. It's in the, uh, the closet..."

"It's in the drawer beside my bed," he cuts in, with a laugh. "Why're you being so weird? I just want to go into my—" His smile fades, and he begins to frown. "Who's in there?"

"I, um—"

"It's my girlfriend, isn't it?"

Her breath lodges in her throat. No, of course not, is what she wants to deny, but the words somehow don't leave her mouth. Her slight moment of hesitation is answer enough, because his expression immediately darkens. Eyes narrowed, jaw clenched, fists tight. He looks angry, angrier than she's ever seen him before, and her heart starts to pound. "Dylan—"

"Step aside, Emma."

Without waiting for her response, he pushes past her and reaches for the door. His hand hovers over the doorknob, and she sees him falter for a second. Although it's dark, she's close enough to him to notice the flicker of plain vulnerability across his face. There is nothing quite like standing on one side of the door, knowing, with absolute certainty, what lies on the other side. It's like wading into deep waters to drown; it's like stepping off a high cliff to fall.

She knows what that's like, as intimately as anyone who's been on this side of the door one too many times before. Her hand moves of its own accord, reaching for him. She wonders, for his sake, if she can stop the inevitable hurt he will have to face once he opens the door.

Chapter 7

"**A**RE YOU ALRIGHT?"

She knows that it's a pointless question, but it slips out of her mouth anyway. Of course, he's not alright. How could anyone be if they caught the person they've been dating since high school fucking around with someone else behind their back?

He's still exactly where she left him, sitting along the sidewalk with his head buried in his arms. Strains of the music from the party echoes down the street, but, thankfully, it's a little more quiet here. At the sound of her voice, he looks up; his eyes tracking her every move as she sets the grocery bag down. He reaches in and pulls out a can, then pops the lid and offers it to her.

"Thanks," she says, a little surprised. She's bought it for him, after all. She starts to sit down, only to falter when he holds out a hand to stop her.

Without saying a word, he shrugs off his football jacket and lays it on the ground beside him. He pats the empty space and reaches for a can of his own. She takes a seat; glancing at him from the corner of her eye. Right now, his mood is mercurial at best, and she's not sure if the littlest thing will set him off. For awhile, they drink in silence, and she watches him chug not one, not two, but three beers at an alarming pace.

Eventually, she hands him her own as well. "You know," she tells him, "a lot of first loves don't last. And relationships that began in high school rarely stand the rest of time. So you shouldn't be so hard on yourself. You gave it your best shot and, like many other high school relationships, it just didn't work out."

He takes a long swig of his beer, and lets out a deep sigh. "I'm not mad about that. I've known that our relationship was over the first time I caught her cheating on me. That was about nine months ago. I'm just disappointed in myself, that I wasted all this time staying with her."

Emma stares at him in surprise. "Why did you?" she can't help but ask.

"Obligation, I guess. Flo's always had a very hard life. Since high school, when her mum left her, she's always been on her own. She lives at my place and if I kicked her out, she'd have nowhere else to go. I've always felt sorry for her but..." he breaks off into a mirthless laugh. "Fuck, I also really hate her right now."

He's been flicking the lid on his can as he speaks, and Emma's a little worried that he'll cut his finger on it, so she reaches forward and stills his hand. She's taken by surprise when he intertwines his fingers with hers.

It's gentle, effortless, comfortable, and it feels like he's been doing it forever.

She blinks and pulls herself together. It's not a big deal, she tells herself, he just needs someone to comfort him. She gives his hand a small squeeze and says, "For what it's worth, I'm really sorry this happened to you. I might not know what you're feeling right now, but I do know what it's like to be in a relationship where the other person doesn't treasure you as much as they should."

He swallows hard and stares down at their inter-locked fingers for a moment. When he looks back up, there's a fire in his eyes that hasn't been there before. And, suddenly, she knows with absolute certainty what he's about to do. She recognizes that look; it makes her breath catch in her throat, and her heart starts to pound in that familiar, yet unfamiliar way it's not done in a very, very long time. She can't look away, she's mesmerized, she wants to close her eyes. He leans forward with a steely determination, and his hand comes up to cup her face; his thumb brushing the curve of cheekbone.

But as his breath glosses her lips, her senses finally kick in.

"I-I don't—" she stutters, turning her face away.

In her peripheral, she notices him freeze. He immediately moves back, and snatches his hand away from hers. That guilty, haunted look on his face cuts straight to her heart. "Right, I'm so sorry—"

"No, don't be. It just seems like you're not thinking very clearly right now and..." she trails off, and lets out a slow breath. "More than anything, I don't want to be the choice you make when you're not sober. I don't want you to be the one you settle for just because you couldn't have her."

"You're not—" he stops and rakes a hand through his hair. He takes a deep breath and sets his beer down, then turns to face her. "I'm not settling. But you're right, I'm also not sober, and it is too soon. I'm really sorry if I made things weird between us."

"You didn't," she hastens to assure him. "And it's not your fault. I don't...I don't have much of a choice myself, so it's not like anything could ever happen between us anyway."

There's a glint in his eye that suggests he knows more than what he lets on. But he doesn't react to that, save to nod. "That's okay. I'll wait." She starts to frown, confused by his words, but he only holds out his hand again. "Still friends?"

"Of course." She grasps his hand, and his grip is steady. Is she imagining it, or does his hand linger around hers? Does his gaze dart down to her lips for a moment?

But it's over in a flash. He picks up his beer, taking a long swig from it as if nothing out of the ordinary just happened. Still, the idea has already been planted in her mind, and she can't help but glance at him again.

Chapter 8

P ALE WHITE SUNLIGHT streams in through the windows, bathing the room in an almost ethereal glow. It's quiet, in the middle of the afternoon, and he's fast asleep.

As quietly as she can, she steals into the room, shutting the door with a soft click behind her. There are a ton of get-well-soon gifts scattered across the table, the dresser and the floor beside the bed. But most of them remain untouched, and she wonders if it's because he isn't interested in opening them, or if they're from people he can no longer remember.

She hopes, for their sake and for his, that it's not the latter.

For a moment, she watches him. His features are relaxed; his eyelashes fanned out on his cheekbones, and his freckles ever more prominent under the light. There are still several bruises marring his skin; his leg is still in a cast and so is his right wrist. But, apart from that, he looks well. He's recovering—physically, at least.

The pang in her chest grows the longer she stares at him, until it's burning, a fiery ache that makes her want to double over. He's forgotten her. Of all people, it had to be her. In the space of his heart that's reserved solely for her, there's only emptiness now. He's forgotten her laughter, his love; their hopes when they first began, their plans for their future; all of their firsts, and all the times he told her that she would be his last love.

Did you really forget how to love me? she wonders, swallowing hard as the thought rises in her mind. What if you never remember how to again?

She takes a deep breath and steps a little closer. There's a small space on the dresser beside his bed, and she reaches into her bag, pulling out a football jacket. For a moment, she hugs it to her chest and squeezes her eyes shut.

She remembers it: navy blue jacket on the grey sidewalk, when he'd first placed it down for her to sit on, their heads light with alcohol and midnight conversation. The soft fabric beneath her bare arms when he eases her down onto it on their fourth date; his lips covering hers with a growing urgency as she pulls his hand underneath her skirt. A blanket of warmth surrounding her as he drapes it over her shoulders at the airport; a small catch in his voice as he says, softly, 'We'll be together again.'

She remembers it all too well. She wishes, desperately, that he'll remember it too.

Carefully, she starts to place it on the dresser. But she must've made a sound, because, suddenly, Dylan wakes up. His gaze fixes on her, bright and clear. And for one moment, a glimmer of hope surges within her. Does he remember...?

But then he blinks, and his eyebrows furrow. "What're you doing back here?"

She falters. This is the first time, she realizes, that they're having a conversation alone. Maybe she can get through to him. "I, uh—I just had something I wanted to give to you," she says, lifting the jacket in her hands. "It's really important."

"Yeah?" There's a suspicious edge to his voice. "Like the other stuff you've been leaving in my room?"

"You know about them?" She'd been so careful, visiting only whenever he's fast asleep. On those days when he's wide awake, she leaves the things with Morgan instead.

"That chemistry textbook, a gift card, a ticket stub and a polaroid of Disneyland?" He points to the window ledge, and that's when she realizes that all the things she's left him are placed there in a neat pile. "Are they really that important?"

"They are if you can remember them."

"The thing is, I can't. That's been made explicitly clear to me by every doctor I've met." With some effort, he pulls himself up into a sitting position. Emma immediately moves forward to help him, but he bats her hand away. "Do you know how frustrating this is? Everyone tells me that there's a huge gap in my memory, but I can't feel it. My memory is perfectly fine to me, and nothing is missing. Everything is good."

With a slow, sinking dread, she realizes what he's trying to tell her. "You're happy with the way things are, aren't you? You won't even try to remember because...you don't want to."

"All I know is that my life is good right now. I have my family with me, and a girlfriend, and my body is recovering. I can't take any of that for granted, and—"

"Wait," she cuts in, with a frown. "You have a girlfriend?"

He nods. "That's why you need to stop whatever it is you're doing. Maybe you and I had something in the past, but I honestly can't remember it anymore. I do remember her though," he adds, a little softer this time. "I remember how I feel about her."

"What—who?" Emma stares at him in utter confusion. Should she get a doctor to check on him again? "Since when did you even have another girlfriend?"

"Not another. One girlfriend." Emma watches with growing disbelief as he presses the emergency button beside his bed. It's just as well—he should really get a nurse to check on his head. At the sound of footsteps, Dylan straightens, his lips lifting in a wide smile. "It's always been her."

Emma turns as the door opens. Her disbelief vanishes, only to be replaced by a slow, dawning shock.

"Florence Aryton?"

Chapter 9

FOR A MOMENT, she can only stare in disbelief at the woman who's just entered the room. It's been years since she last saw Florence Aryton, so the memory she has is quite different from the one standing in front of her.

Florence during their college days had sported rebellious red hair, black jackets and leather boots, and rode a motorcycle with flawless ease in direct defiance of every head cheerleader stereotype. This Florence, on the other hand, looks demure and calm, her light brown hair tucked into a neat bun, and her nurse's outfit and scrubs donned with professional perfection.

"Flo," Dylan says, and there's a brightness in his voice that makes Emma's heart twist. He sits up just a bit straighter and grins at her. "Sorry to have to call you here, I know how busy you are."

"Not at all," Flo says, as she crosses the room and removes her scrubs along the way. She shoves them into the pocket of her uniform and smiles at Emma. "Hi. I'm the nurse assigned to this ward. And you are?"

Emma studies her for a second or two. She can't tell if Flo genuinely doesn't remember her, or is pretending not to. Then again, Emma wasn't exactly anyone special back then, so she gives Flo the benefit of the doubt. "I'm Emma."

She doesn't take the hand that Flo offers to her, but Flo reaches out and shakes her hand anyway. A cool, firm handshake that Emma immediately drops. "You must be one of Dylan's friends," remarks Flo.

I'm his girlfriend, damn it, Emma wants to snap, but at the same time, she won't. The doctors have been very clear about what it means to have retrograde amnesia. Telling a patient facts about their life wouldn't make those facts true if said patient doesn't recall or believe them.

Case in point: her relationship, or now lack thereof, with Dylan.

Thankfully, before she can come up with an answer, Dylan speaks first. "She seems to think that we're something more than that," he explains to Flo. "But I don't remember her. I just remember you."

Flo meets Emma's gaze for a moment, before she looks away. There's a flicker of something—it's over in a flash, but Emma catches it anyway. And, suddenly, she understands. "He remembers you," she repeats, studying Flo carefully. "And you haven't done anything to clear that up, have you?"

Flo blinks. "What would I have to clear up?"

"He doesn't remember what came after. And you have no intention of letting him know, do you?"

"What came after?" Dylan asks, plain confusion in his voice.

"You two broke up," Emma declares, at the same time as Flo says, "Nothing." There's a moment's pause as Dylan looks between the two of them, like a poor spectator lost in an unwinnable tennis match, before Emma repeats, in disbelief, "Nothing?"

Flo averts her eyes.

A surge of anger rises within Emma, too strong to stop, and she turns back to Dylan. "She's lying to you—"

"That was—" Flo starts, but Emma ignores her.

"She's obviously taking advantage of the state you're in and lying to you. She knows that you remember her, and that you'll believe anything she tells you, and that's why she won't tell you the truth—"

"Don't talk like that about Flo," Dylan cuts in, his voice sharp. "When I woke up, everyone was telling me different versions of my life, including you. Everytime I had a visitor, they told me something new about myself that I'd never known before until my life looked like this huge, jumbled mess. Flo was the only one who told me things I could remember, so if you don't mind, I'm choosing to believe her."

Emma lets out an incredulous laugh. "So you'd rather believe the words of one person, instead of everyone else's?"

"Yes, because Flo's my girlfriend."

"She's not your girlfriend!" Emma's voice rises in frustration, and Dylan's eyes narrow. He starts to get up, tugging on the drip attached to his arm, but Flo quickly pushes him back down and readjusts the tubes.

"You really shouldn't upset him like that," she tells Emma. "He'll only get hurt." Emma opens her mouth, ready to argue, but Flo looks down when her pager beeps. "I have to get back to work," she says to Dylan. "Will you be okay?"

He sighs and runs his uninjured hand through his hair. "I'll be fine. Just take her out with you."

Emma frowns. "But—"

"You should leave," Flo tells her calmly. "Come on."

Emma stares at Dylan, then Flo, and back at Dylan once more. But neither of them seem willing to meet her gaze or back down. With a frustrated huff, she grabs her bag and the jacket she'd meant to leave him, and storms out of the room. As soon as the door shuts behind them, she whirls around on Flo. "You won't be able to get away with this."

"Maybe," Flo accedes. "But, until then, I'm still the one he loves."

She walks off without a backward glance, and Emma stares at her departing figure, too angry to think of a parting retort. How did things come to this? Was it her fault for not staying by Dylan's side to remind him of her existence? But then, even if she did, what use would that be? She could swear to the moon and back that she was his girlfriend, and he still wouldn't believe her, because he didn't remember her.

And it wasn't even out of character for him to act like this. Even before the accident, Dylan never wavered or faltered. He stuck staunchly to the things he believed in, even when the whole world said otherwise.

The only difference then, was that he believed in her.

If I can't make him believe me... A thought suddenly comes to her mind and she reaches for the doorknob. How hadn't she thought of this before? If I can't make him believe me, he'll have to believe himself.

"What're you doing back here?" Dylan asks when she steps back into the room. His eyes narrow and he starts to reach for the emergency button. "I told you to leave."

She walks right up to him and drops his jacket down on the dresser. "I didn't want to rush you before, because I know you're still recuperating," she says, ignoring his orders. "But your mom told me that you'll be able to remove your bandages in two weeks."

"What does that have to do—"

"When you remove your wrist brace, you'll know which one of us is lying—Flo or I."

He blinks, then stares down at his right hand, where the brace is covered all the way up to his thumb, and down his forearm. He's had a bad fracture there, and she almost kicks herself for not thinking of it sooner.

This is the only proof he really needs.

"What's on my wrist?" he asks at last, an equal mix of suspicion and curiosity in his voice.

"Remove the brace," she tells him calmly, "and then you'll find out."

She turns to leave, but his voice stops her. "Wait," he says, reaching for the jacket that she left on the dresser. "You forgot about this."

She meets his gaze squarely. "That's yours."

Without waiting for his reply, she leaves the room. There's no use staying when he doesn't want her around. Until he removes his wrist brace, he'll never willingly be hers.

And even then, maybe not.

Chapter 10

"HEY, EMMA, HOLD up!"

She falters in her steps and glances over her shoulder. A sting of guilt tightens in her chest as she watches Dylan race down the steps with her suitcase in hand. But as soon as he draws near, she resumes her pace again. He keeps up with his long strides, and she feels his gaze on her.

"What's the rush?" he asks, after a moment's silence.

"No rush. It's just nice to finally leave the hospital."

"I'm glad you're alright now," he says, with a warm smile. "Do you need a ride?"

She shakes her head. "I'll just get a cab."

"Are you sure? My car's parked just across the street."

"No, I have to get to the hotel my parents are staying at. It'll just be out of the way for you."

He must have sensed something in her voice, because he doesn't push. "Okay, then," he says, and passes her suitcase back to her.

Their fingers unexpectedly brush, and Emma quickly snatches her hand back. Her cheeks warm, and she looks down at her feet. "Thanks."

"No problem."

"Seriously, thank you," she says, glancing up again, only to find him already staring at her. She fights the urge to look away, and meets his gaze steadily. "For everything."

There's a beat; a silent current of understanding—she knows that he knows exactly what she means. He nods without a word; his lips curving into a small smile. She tightens her grip on her suitcase and starts to head down the steps.

"Hey, Emma." His voice stops her. She turns back in surprise. For a moment or two, he seems to falter. He runs a hand through his hair, and starts, haltingly, "Do you want to give things a try?"

She blinks. "What?"

"Between us, I mean, you and I." Her eyes widen, and he hesitates again for a bit, before he continues on. "I know the circumstances and the timing aren't perfect. You just got out of a traumatic relationship a few weeks ago, and I had my first breakup some months back. And now you're leaving when summer ends, and I'll be stuck here for the foreseeable future."

She frowns, a little unsure where he's going with this. If he's making a list of all the reasons for them not to be together, he's doing an excellent job at it.

"But I really like you," he says. "I think you're smart and kind and pretty, and in all these months as lab partners, we never run out of things to talk about. And if these past few weeks have proven anything, it's that you already know me better than anyone else. I know this probably won't amount to anything, but I also know that it'll be the biggest regret in my life if I don't at least try to let you know how I feel so..." he trails off and bites his lip, looking right at her. "What do you think?"

She stares at him for a moment. His eyes are bright with hope; a million shades of sunlight threaded in his hair. He reminds her of the first light of spring;

of hardened hearts melting softly into new green be-
ginnings.

She takes a deep breath and heads back up the
stairs, one by one, until she's standing on leveled
ground with him. "Here," she says, pushing her suitcase towards him, "hold this."

Once her suitcase is in his hands, she leans up and
kisses him.

It takes him by surprise. She can feel the way he
tenses beneath her; and she knows that if she didn't
have her eyes closed, she would find his wide and
open. She lingers for a brief second, then pulls away,
tipping back on her heels to gaze up at him.

They're still close enough that she can count the
freckles on his cheeks, and the flecks of green in his
brown eyes. He smiles, warm and light and full of
hope, and asks, "Is that a yes?"

She smiles, just as bright as him, and nods.

He sets her bag down at their feet, then frames
her face between his hands and kisses her. Soft and
gentle at first, the way she'd kissed him earlier, and
then, when she leans into him, heavy and deeply.
A slow heat rises between them, and she is utterly
aware of him. He tastes of the candy they shared
earlier in the hospital; and there are calluses on his

thumb when he brushes her cheek. She grips onto his jacket and opens her mouth beneath his; her mind spinning with his kisses and the heady realization that everything about this is brand new.

The start of every relationship must be like this, she thinks, in the back of her mind, where you learn minute details about the other person that you've never noticed before.

And she can't wait to discover them all.

Chapter 11

"WHERE ARE WE going?"

At her question, he shoots her a glance over his shoulder and grins. "What part of 'it's a surprise' don't you get?" he says, tugging her along when she falters.

"The surprise part," she admits. "You know I'm not good with those. If it's anything too big or scary, you're not going to have the reaction you were hoping for."

"Don't look so worried, it's honestly not that big a deal. Here we are," he says, pulling her to a halt in front of a shop.

She blinks at the big neon sign on the storefront. "You brought me to a tattoo place?"

"Yes."

"Are you making me get a tattoo?"

He laughs at that. "No, but you're welcome to if you want one. Preferably somewhere only I know about," he adds teasingly, and they're in that stage of a relationship where the slightest innuendo makes her blush. He smirks at that, and holds the door open for her. "No, I'm the one getting a tattoo. I had to book a slot because this place is pretty popular."

She nods and looks around at the art on the wall, and the various tattoo designs on display, while he checks in at the counter. When he returns, he pulls her towards the empty space on the bench. They sit for a moment or two in silence, with only the echo of faint buzzing in the background, until she can't stop her curiosity. "What're you going to get?"

"I don't know," he says with a shrug. He studies the designs on the wall for a few seconds, before he asks, "What do you think about the head of Medusa on my chest?"

She stares at him, torn between amusement and horror. Given his totally straight face, she can't for the life of her decide whether he's joking or not. "I, uh.. .well, it's your choice and I respect that. I'll probably have to blindfold my eyes or something, or we'll have to do it in the dark, just so I won't get nightmares."

He chuckles. "I was only joking," he says, to her relief. "But I'll admit, I'm kind of tempted to get it now that I know how accommodating you'll be."

She rolls her eyes at him, and he winks back—a silent banter that only the two of them understand. In the back of her mind, she wishes desperately to capture this moment: the gleam in his eyes, the curve of his lips, sunlight threaded in his hair. She wants to close her eyes to remember it, but every second she closes her eyes means a little less time to look at him.

He must've noticed her smile fading, because he suddenly frowns. "What's wrong?"

She looks down at her lap, picking at her nails for awhile. "What do you think of Linville?"

"You mean our rival college?" She nods, and his frown deepens. "It's pretty much the same as Riverton, except as football captain I'm obliged to say that their football team's shit. Why do you ask?"

"They have a solid curriculum, like the one I took at Riverton. I probably won't have much trouble catching up, coming out ahead even."

"Emma." His voice is quiet; the look on his face serious. "Are you trying to tell me that you want to go to Linville instead?"

"Well, it's not a bad school..."

"Anything less than your dream school which you worked so hard to get into, and actually qualified for, is a bad school because you're settling. And I told you before: don't settle."

"I know!" She runs a hand through her hair and lets out a deep sigh. "It's just that...things between us are so good, you know? I want to find out where things go from here, but I'll never be able to if I leave."

"What're you talking about? You leaving is exactly how we'll find out where things will go from here. Whether we'll make long distance work, or whether we'll go our separate ways—we'll only ever know if you leave."

"But..." She bites her lip at the look of hope on his face—and shit, she really hates to do this to him, but one of them needs to be realistic at least. "Long distance relationships never work out, Dylan."

His lips quirk in a faint smile that's a little sad. "Do you really have that little faith in me?"

"No, of course not, I trust you! But no one I know has ever made long distance work, and we've only been dating for a month."

He shrugs."Flo and I started dating when we were fifteen and look how that turned out." He seems to sense that she's not really convinced, because he sighs and pulls her closer towards him. He sits at an angle and tucks her knees between both of his, so that they're directly facing each other. "Be honest," he says gently, "hand over heart, this school is your dream, yes?"

She nods.

"Then go chase it. Attend your classes, graduate as valedictorian—which I know you will, and take time to consider your job offers. And then you can decide whether you want to continue living there, or come home to me, or we can even make a new home halfway."

She blinks back sudden tears and gives him a watery smile. "That's in the middle of the ocean."

He cups her cheek and brushes away a stray tear with his thumb. "We'll make it work," he says, and pulls her into his arms. She tucks her head beneath his chin and closes her eyes. For a moment, they stay like that, with his arms around her shoulders and his pulse steady against her skin. She breathes him in and hopes that his words will come true.

She hopes they'll last.

After awhile, he pulls away and reaches into his bag. "Here," he tells her, as he draws out a pen and a piece of paper. "Write your name on this."

"What for?"

"For my tattoo," he explains, and raises his eyebrows at her. "You didn't really think I'd have the head of Medusa on my chest, did you? Your name in your handwriting," he adds, tracing a line across his right wrist, "I want it here, so I have something to remember you by."

A wide smile spreads across her face—he's so ridiculously cheesy sometimes, but no one has ever made her smile the way he has. "You could have a lock of my hair," she teases.

"Are we living in medieval times?" he shoots back.

A small laugh escapes her at that, and he grins and pulls her close again. He places the pen and paper onto her lap, and presses his lips against the side of her forehead, so that she can feel his lips against her as he speaks.

"Your name on my skin," he murmurs in a low voice that only she can hear, "I never want to forget you."

She lifts her head and meets his gaze for a moment. There's not a trace of teasing or irony on his face, so she smiles and picks up the pen. She must've written her name a hundred times before, but this feels like the first.

Emma. Every loop, every line, every letter has a new meaning—her name will be indelible; she can't ever be forgotten.

Chapter 12

A S SHE REACHES the room, a wave of uncertainty fills her. Morgan had been more than vague on the other end of the line when she'd called. Something about Dylan wanting to meet with her as soon as she's able to.

She doesn't know if that's a good or bad thing. She does so hate surprises.

For a moment, she falters, with one hand on the doorknob. She hasn't been to the hospital for three weeks, nor has she heard from Dylan until now. His family has given her regular updates, but nothing about their news remotely suggests that he's even thought about her, much less remembered her.

She doesn't want to get her hopes up, only to have them fall apart with the bitter taste of reality.

"Hey." The familiar voice comes from behind her, and she whirls around. Dylan is several feet away, in a wheelchair pushed by a nurse who isn't Flo. He glances back at the nurse and says, "It's okay, I can wheel myself in from here."

The nurse nods and heads off, leaving an awkward silence in her wake. Emma shifts on her feet; feeling terribly out of her depth. She's not sure what kind of mercurial mood he's in today, and the last thing she wants is for things to end on a sour note the way it had before.

"Hi," she says at last.

"Have a seat," he tells her, gesturing to the empty bench just outside the room. She hesitates, then slowly settles down on it. He wheels himself a little bit closer, and that's when she realizes what she's been missing.

"You removed your wrist brace."

He nods. "It took more than two weeks for the doctors to take it off. Apparently, I've injured it before so it took longer than they expected to heal."

"Back to back injuries—once in your senior year of high school, and then in freshman year of college," she tells him. "Both times playing football."

"Dad told me the same thing." There's another pause, before he says, unexpectedly, "I'd like to apologise."

Her eyes flicker up to his; hope tight in her chest.

"It's not that I didn't want to believe you guys. You, Mom, Dad, Morgan, my colleagues from work, my newer friends. It's just that..." He runs a hand through his hair, and lets out a slow breath. "When I woke up, I felt very lost and scared. In my head, I was still in high school and everything was perfect. But then I looked into the mirror, and saw this much older guy staring back at me, and I—I knew something didn't fit, but I didn't know what. And then people would come into my room, one after another, and talk to me as if they knew me their whole lives. But to me, they're all just strangers. Almost everyone apart from my family was a stranger, except for Flo, so I believed her because, at least, what she said made sense."

"What did she tell you?" Emma asks quietly.

"All she says is that she still cares a lot about me, even after all these years. In my memory, she's my girlfriend so I call her that, and she doesn't ever say that she's not, either. But she's really not, is she? Otherwise I wouldn't have this."

He turns his right hand with his palm faced up. The letters—emma—are still there, indelible ink on his skin, unaffected by the accident and his amnesia. Even if his mind can't remember, and his heart won't remember, his body will. She is etched on his skin, within his cells, between his veins.

Unable to stop herself, she leans forward and, with a shaking hand, traces the word on his wrist. Tears rise to her eyes, and she swallows hard. This is like waiting for rain after a long drought, and it has finally come.

Even if it's only a drizzle, she'll take it.

She starts to pull away, but he catches her hand. His eyes rove her features; a flicker of curiosity on his face. He's studying her, she realizes. To him, she's a stranger that he's looking at properly for the first time.

"Emma," he breathes, quiet and wondering, "who are you?" His fingers curl around hers in a steady grip—where before he was her lifeline, now, she is his. He pulls her a little closer and she follows, right to the edge of her seat, so that her knees brush his. His gaze is still magnetic, drawing her in, drowning her deep. She can't look away. "Tell me about yourself."

Her lips finally lift into a small smile. This is the first step. "What would you like to know?"

He opens his mouth to respond, but a voice cuts in right at that moment. "Dylan? What're you two doing?" Emma glances to the left; her heart sinking.

It's Flo.

Chapter 13

THE SURPRISED BEAT of silence seems to last for an eternity. Then, because Dylan still hasn't let go of her hand, Emma moves back a little. It's not until then that she realizes how close they were—with her knees between his, and his face close enough that she can see the small scar on his neck from the accident.

But Dylan doesn't let her go. If anything, he pulls her right back, and places her hand over his knee. She almost startles at the contact—the warmth of his hand; the rough skin from the scrapes on his knee. Fuck, she's really missed him. It's everything she can do not to wrap her arms around him, but Flo is there.

"Emma and I were talking," Dylan says to Flo, without once looking away from Emma.

"Is that so?" Flo's gaze lands on their hands, and Emma doesn't miss the way the other woman's features harden. Flo turns to Emma and says, "Can I speak with you for a moment?"

Emma stares at her, not sure where Flo's going with this. Finally, she nods and starts to rise, but Dylan's hand tightens around hers. She looks down at him, only to see the silent plea in his eyes. Don't go.

Now that he's stopped believing in Flo, she's the one he clings to.

"It's okay," she tells him, with a small smile, and he reluctantly lets go. She follows Flo down the hallway, until Dylan is out of sight. Flo starts to head down yet another hallway, but Emma stops her. "We can talk here."

"Okay, then." Flo nods and leans back against the wall. Everything about her is calculated—from her relaxed posture, to the leveled look in her eyes. And Emma is struck by the sudden memory that this is the Flo she remembered from college—cool and calm, bold and defiant, whose confidence Emma had once admired so deeply.

"I know what you've been doing," Flo says. "You've been leaving mementos for him to remember you by. But you know that won't work, right? Amnesia doesn't just vanish because of a trigger, no matter how big or memorable it is."

"I know," Emma returns quietly. "I didn't leave them for him to remember me. I left them for him so that even if he didn't want me to visit, I'd still be on his mind. It was important, especially because you were lying to him the whole time."

"I never told him that I was his girlfriend."

"You never told him you weren't. You let him think whatever he wanted to think, so it was still a lie by omission."

Flo stares at her for a long moment, before she lets out a sigh. "Fine, so I didn't tell him the truth. It was wrong of me, and I know that. But," she adds, in a quieter voice this time, "it's only because I really need him."

"Then you've never really loved him, have you? Even back in high school and college, you've only ever needed him."

"Is that so wrong?" Flo fires back. "I still care a lot about him—I always have. You wouldn't understand what it's like to be as alone as I have been. Back in high school, my mum left and Dylan was the only one I had. And now my dad is very sick, and along comes Dylan, and he remembers me. He loves me despite what I did to him in the past, and I just—" she breaks off and looks down at her feet. "It's like everything I lost has come back to me, and I don't want to let go this time."

Emma falls silent; her mind reeling. She doesn't know what to say to that. Flo takes a step forward, meeting Emma's gaze squarely, and when she speaks, her voice is soft. "I just want to have him, for a little while, so that I won't always have to be alone."

Emma swallows hard. "He's not an object, like a teddy bear that we can share. He's his own person, and—" She lets out a slow breath. As she looks at Flo, she realizes, then, that there is no 'other woman'. There are only two women: the past called Flo and the present called Emma, and there's no knowing what the future holds. "With or without amnesia, he's capable of making his own decisions, and I've always respected the ones he's made."

"What're you saying?"

"It's up to him to make his own decision, whether it's you, or me, or neither of us. I will accept whatever decision he makes. And if you really care about him, you'll do the same."

Without waiting for Flo's response, she turns on her heels and leaves. Her heart is in her throat and her chest is tight, and every step she takes farther away from Dylan leaves her empty inside. But this is what she intends to do: to accept his choice, no matter how painful the outcome may be, and never look back.

This is her choice.

Now she'll wait for his.

Chapter 14

"HAVE YOU HEARD?" The rumours make their way over to her, even when she does her best to ignore them. She reaches for her earphones, only to pause when the person continues, excitement clear in their voice, "Dylan's breaking up with Flo right now."

Oh.

Her feet come to a halt. A group of freshmen hurries past her, chattering and giggling along the way. She bites her lip and hesitates. She is headed in that direction—it's the closest exit to the parking lot anyway, but does she really want to witness their breakup? She watches a few more students rush past her in the same direction as the freshmen.

Oh, screw it, she does.

She takes a deep breath and follows them. It's really just the most convenient way, she tells herself, as she turns the corner. Already, there's a babble of noise in the background, but above all is the sound of wretched sobs.

"—it was a mistake! A terrible, terrible mistake, but you have to believe me..."

As the person in front of her moves aside, she finally catches a glimpse of the scene that's making everyone watch with wide eyes and slack jaws. To say that Florence Aryton looks like a mess is an understatement. Tears and mascara stream down her face as she sobs openly, and when she drags a hand through her hair, she somehow manages to make it even more frazzled than before.

Dylan, on the other hand, is the epitome of calm in the face of a storm. He's standing in an almost defensive posture, with his arms folded across his chest. Every now and then, he glances over at the crowd, then back at Flo. It's clear that he's aware a crowd has gathered around them to watch, and seems utterly uncomfortable with the attention.

"I believe you." Dylan's voice is low, if a bit strangled. "It's just something that I can't let slide. Not when it's happened three times."

Emma blinks in surprise. Based on what Dylan's told her, she only knows that it happened once before. But three times? Briefly, she wonders how someone as intelligent and honest as him can put up with that. Then again, she reminds herself, you of all people should know how much a person can tolerate if they really want to.

The gasps and murmurs grow at Dylan's revelation, and she can understand perfectly why. It is a big deal that the football captain and head cheerleader are breaking up. They were the cliché; the star couple; each other's first loves; high school sweethearts—but now that illusion has been shattered.

For a moment, she wonders what everyone would think if they found out that the other couple they believed in—the one where the bad boy fell madly in love with the good girl—was all a lie too.

She lets out a slow breath and pulls herself together. When she focuses back on the scene at hand, Flo is still crying. "—we were drunk that first time, Dyl, it didn't mean anything! That second time was a mistake, just a mistake—"

"A mistake?" someone from the crowd echoes mockingly. "You mean you accidentally began riding him because you thought he was a horse?"

There are degrading laughs at this, but one sharp look from Dylan makes them fall silent. He sweeps a warning glance across the crowd, as though daring them to say anything more. And then, suddenly, his gaze lands on her.

Emma freezes. Is he really looking at her, or some-one behind her? His gaze is steady and clear, so much like the night they almost kissed. A familiar heat rises to her cheeks and she looks away.

"Hey, Torres!"

Vince Raillor pushes his way through the crowd like he owns the whole damn school. She's been to enough football games to know that he's a liability to the team. Whenever he plays, he loses more often than he wins, and so he's benched half the season, but he still acts like he's God's gift to the world. Greg Simmons—head of the notorious frat Corvus—has an arm around Vince's shoulder. Then there's Callum Wright, the one she saw at the party, looking bored as hell but still having his friends' backs regardless, and that's why she's always so wary of him. The devil with a charming smirk, Keith Jacobs, rounds out the group, surveying the scene before him with a general air of amusement.

Fresh tension fills the atmosphere at their arrival, and, immediately, several of Dylan's friends move forward. Meanwhile, her breath catches in her throat, and her gaze instinctively flits towards the nearest exit. But the crowd is pressed so close that there's no way for her to squeeze through without being utterly noticeable.

A hush falls over the crowd as Vince stops right in front of Dylan. He tries to stare Dylan down, but the latter only meets his gaze without flinching. "What the hell are you doing to my girl?" Vince demands sharply.

"I'm not your girl—" Flo starts weakly, but Dylan's voice, calm and quiet, cuts in before she can say anything else.

"I was always under the impression that we didn't own them. I don't know what kind of backward, Neanderthal way of thinking you have, but I've no intention of dropping my pants and pissing all over just to mark my territory. If you want to be with her, ask her. But that's no longer my problem because Flo and I aren't dating anymore."

Flo's features begin to crumple. "You don't mean that—"

But Vince steps up to Dylan; a deep-set scowl on his face. "Don't talk down to me, you shit," he growls. "You're just sore about it because she knows that I'm a better fuck than you ever were. And now you're playing the victim just because you couldn't get it up—"

Dylan moves so quickly that Emma almost doesn't catch it. One moment he and Vince are standing eye to eye; the next Dylan slams Vince against the nearest row of lockers. Vince's friends immediately move forward, only to be stopped by other guys in football jackets.

For the first time, she sees Dylan's anger. His eyes are narrowed; his jaw set. He presses an arm down on Vince's chest to keep the latter from moving, but even then—even then, he doesn't hit Vince. He keeps his anger in check with his other hand curled into a fist, and he swallows several times before speaking.

"It's not enough that you fucked my girlfriend three times," he snarls. "But you fucked her in my house, on my bed, and sent pictures to the football team to brag about it. I tried not to make a scene by breaking up with her in private," he adds, throwing a glare at

Flo over his shoulder, who seems to shrink at his words. "But she followed me, crying about how I was unfair to her, when she was the one who asked for exclusivity in our relationship. And now you dare to put your filthy presense in my line of vision, and tell me that having sex with Flo is a competition you've won. And maybe you're right—maybe you've won. Because you clearly have as massive a dick as you're behaving right now, and you feel the need to stroke your own ego by humiliating someone else. But you will dig deep into that black hole you call your heart, and show me some fucking respect because I am your captain. And if you make one more move or sound to piss me off, I will make you regret it."

A stunned silence reigns in the wake of his words. Dylan moves away from Vince and turns to Flo, who stares up at him with wide eyes. "And you," he continues, a little quieter now. "I'll give you a week to move your things out of my place. There're a couple of rooms on campus if you want, or I can pull some strings and get you an apartment elsewhere. But I don't want to see or speak to you unless necessary."

Flo lets out a choked sob and reaches for Dylan, but he sidesteps her and turns to leave. As if on second thought, he suddenly stops and glances back.

"I accept your apology, and I think that, in time, I could come to forgive you," he tells her. His voice is quiet, and if Emma weren't standing within that part of the crowd, she would've missed it entirely. "But I'll never forget what you did, or the hurt that you caused me." A flicker of vulnerability crosses his face— so similar to the one that Emma saw on him that night of the party—but it's over in a flash. "Goodbye, Flo."

He turns to leave, with several of his friends following, and the crowd automatically parts for them. As he draws near, Emma finds herself holding her breath. Somehow, she's not surprised when his gaze locks on hers. That spark in his eyes is back; one corner of his lips lift in a hint of a smile. It's a discreet action that no one else seems to notice; secret that's just between them.

She very nearly smiles.

As Dylan and his friends leave, the rest of the crowd begins to disperse, and Emma heads for the parking lot. But something in her peripheral vision catches her eye, and her feet come to a halt. She looks up over to the right, where Vince and his friends are still talking among themselves. But there's one person who stands apart, and he's looking directly at her.

Keith.

He doesn't react, save to raise one eyebrow. Not a silent question; a mocking gesture. Her heart leaps to her throat and she quickly spins on her heels and leaves. Surely, surely, he hasn't noticed the interaction between her and Dylan? She's safe, isn't she?

Chapter 15

"**S**HIT."

The curse slips out of her mouth before she can stop herself, and even though it's muffled, he seems to hear it anyway. In an instant, he's leaning over her shoulder and reaching for her hand. "What's wrong?"

"Nothing," she says, pulling her hand away from his. "I just accidentally burnt myself, that's all."

"That's all?" he repeats incredulously. "Come on, I'm taking you to the nurse's office. If you don't take care of it, you'll blister and scar."

The hard glint in his eyes makes her suspect that he won't take no for an answer. So, after he's told their professor what happened, she follows him out of the lab and down the hallway. She hasn't really noticed it before, but he's quite tall. Almost half a head taller than Keith, and Keith is no slouch himself. His hair is almost bronze under the sunlight that flits in through the opened windows, and she feels like a lost little puppy as she trails behind him in his shadow.

Her feet come to a halt when she notices the nurse's office sign. "Wait." He stops and shoots her a glance over his shoulder, and she shrugs. "I think I'll go to the bathroom instead."

"Emma—"

She sidesteps him when he reaches out to stop her. "It's just a small burn, honestly," she says, as she heads for the nearest washroom. "Once I rinse my hand under cold water, I'll be fine. You'll see."

"Fine, then use the accessible one." He points her to the sole bathroom between the men's and women's. "That way I can make sure you're doing a proper job of it."

She falters for a moment, then squares her shoulders and steps into the accessible bathroom. He steps in after her, and the door swings shut behind them. She starts to wonder what will happen if someone notices them stepping into a bathroom together, but then sets her worries aside.

For now, there's a much bigger issue to worry about.

She flips on the tap and starts to run her hand under cold water. And all the while she is very, very aware of him—watching her every move. After a few minutes, the reddish swell on her hand has started to subside, and it no longer hurts. She turns off the tap and reaches for the paper towels.

Then she falters.

In the next second, his hand closes over her arm. "I knew it." His voice is so soft that she can barely hear it, but the hint of anger threaded through every syllable is there—plain and deafening in the silence. "I wondered why you always wore sweaters during the summer. People have been talking about it, and I knew—I guessed..."

Her breath lodges in her throat as he slowly, gently, turns her wrist. With his other hand, he tugs her sleeve up, so that her lower arm is completely exposed. Laid bare.

And the angry purple bruises are there, like deadly orchids blooming on her skin.

With a sharp breath, she twists away from him and tugs her sleeve back down. Her heart is racing, pounding, in her throat, and her face is hot with fresh humiliation. He's her lab partner—the easy-going, quick-witted boy who seems to admire her not because she's the girlfriend of a football player, but because she's terribly intelligent and formidable in her own right. And because of that, he's the last person she wants to know about this.

"Who?" he demands, his voice still deadly quiet. Calm. Too calm, like hell before it's unleashed. "Is it someone in your family?"

Her eyes go wide and she whirls around on him. "How could you even think that? My parents would give up their entire business and move if I ever so much as hinted that I wanted them here! They miss me more than I can even put in words, and they would never do something like this!"

"So it's him then." He pins her with a steady gaze, and she finds herself unable to look away. "It's Keith?"

She drags in a deep breath, prepared to lie through her teeth, only to find that she can't do it. She can't lie this time—not when he's looking at her with such soft sympathy, not when his hand is wrapped around her arm in such a gentle grip, gentler than anything she's ever felt before.

"Emma," he says quietly, when she remains silent. "Let me help you."

She bites down on the inside of her cheek, hard enough to taste blood. He's holding out a life buoy to her amidst drowning waters, and it takes everything in her not to reach out and grab it. "If you really want to help me," she says instead, "don't tell anyone."

She pulls her arm out of his grasp, ready to leave, but he only steps into her path. There's a knowing glint in his eyes as he asks, "What does Keith have on you to make you stay?"

Damn him. He really is too clever for his own good. Without looking at him, she turns on her heels and walks away. But all the while, her chest is tight with unease at having rejected the only person who's ever offered her help. She's made the right choice, hasn't she? Hasn't she?

Chapter 16

THE DAISIES ON the windowsill are the only things left in the otherwise empty study. Briefly, she considers taking it along with her, but—no, she won't. That once belonged to him. What's hers she'll take, what's his she'll leave behind, and what's their s...

Those things, like their future, are still left hanging in the air.

"Are you sure this is what you want?" A voice breaks her out from her thoughts, and she glances up. Scout is standing by the doorway of the study, with the last of Emma's boxes in her arms. "He'll be disappointed if he comes back and finds that you're not here."

Emma smiles a little. In the past twelve hours since she's left the hospital, she's had plenty of time to think. And this, she's certain, is the right decision. "It's not like I'm leaving the country. Not even the state. It's just really hard being alone in this house without him. If he ever wants to find me, his family knows that I'm moving in with you and Dave."

"Actually, you're moving in with the baby," Scout says, with a teasing smile. "I hope you're prepared to wake up at three in the middle of the night to do a diaper change."

"Somehow, I feel like you're secretly happy that I'm moving in," Emma remarks. Scout grins, and she knows that she's hit the nail on the head. Her best friend will shamelessly use her as a babysitter, and Emma, as godmother, will only be happy to be made use of. Emma closes the door to the study and follows Scout back to the living room, where the rest of the boxes are.

"Anyway," Emma continues, as they start taping up the boxes, "if there's one thing that Dylan's taught me, it's to never settle for anything less than I deserve. And, right now, I don't deserve to have to put my life on hold. I've done that for almost a month now—I'm on sabbatical from work, I don't eat properly, I don't sleep well. Every day, I worry about him; and every night, I think about him. I'm not going to stop loving him but... I have to move on, somehow, right? I can't put 'pause' on my life forever, because everything else is still in 'play'."

Scout nods slowly. "You're right, of course," she says, before she frowns in thought. "But, you know, if you'd fought Flo a little bit more, maybe you could've gotten him back."

"Maybe. But then, even if I did, I don't think it would be real," Emma says quietly. "Whether he remembers me or not, he has to choose me because he wants to. Not because he feels obligated by our past, or because he doesn't have Flo or anyone else. It has to be because it's me."

Scout offers her an understanding smile. "I can assure you, he'd be an idiot not to." She picks up another box, only for a stack of books to tumble out. "My bad," she says, as they start to shove the books back into the box again. "Are those our old textbooks?"

"Yes, from high school, I think."

"I haven't seen them in forever. Why do you even keep those?"

"Sentimental value?" Emma suggests. She's actually not even very sure. "I think I have a habit of keeping way too many things."

"Yes, but sentimentality towards textbooks? Have you forgotten how horrifying exams used to be?"

"I actually really liked exams. They were the best part of school."

"Boo, you nerd." Scout rolls her eyes and throws one of the books at Emma, who catches it with a grin. A piece of paper slips out of the book and flutters to the floor, and Scout reaches for it. "What's this?"

"Not sure. Is that one of my notes?"

"Emma, meet me by the benches after school," Scout reads aloud, before handing the note back to Emma. "Who's it from? Dylan?"

She shakes her head. "No, my ex. I must've left it in the textbook by accident—I didn't think I kept anything from him." She starts to rip the note down the middle and—

Wait.

A sudden thought occurs to her, and she opens the note again. Something about it seems terribly familiar. But what...? She reads it once, then twice, and then she realizes what it is. "Where's my phone?"

"Your phone?" Scout glances around, then grabs it from the coffee table. "Here."

Emma unlocks her phone and goes straight to her photos. Just a few weeks ago, she'd taken a picture of the slip of paper—the one that the police had found with Dylan.

She holds them up side by side: the note that had been slotted into her textbook back in high school, and the other that had been with Dylan the day of the accident.

"The handwriting," breathes Scout, as she peers over Emma's shoulder to get a better look.

It's exactly the same.

Chapter 17

S LATE GREY WALLS and threadbare furniture create an atmosphere of doom and gloom, but somehow, it's fitting at a time like this.

It's fitting for him.

It's been years since she last saw Keith Jacobs. Just like Scout, who remembers her ex as he was, and not as he is now, Emma thinks of Keith the same way. Crew cut, wide grin, broad shoulders. She remembers his dark hair gleaming in the sunlight, a fitting white shirt over his tanned muscles, a football tucked under his arm. She also remembers his lips twisted into a cold, hard smirk, a taunting gleam in his eyes, and his hand curled into a fist.

For a moment, she falters outside the room. This is Keith, not as she remembers, but of the present day. If anything, his years in prison seem to have done him good. He looks bigger, stronger, taller now, slouched in his seat with his long legs sprawled out beneath the table. She'd give anything for Dylan to be here now. But then, she'd also give anything for him not to be anywhere near Keith, ever, in this lifetime and all others.

I can do this.

She takes a deep breath and steps into the room. There are cameras around, security is watching, and she's no longer the Emma he once knew either. Keith glances up, and one corner of his lips lift in a hint of a smirk. "It's been awhile."

She settles down opposite him and folds her hands in her lap. "Not long enough."

"Are you here to gloat?"

"Yes, actually. You should've really used your time in prison more wisely. Learning how to improve your penmanship, for starters. Instead, you still behave the exact same way: violent, reckless and stupid enough to use the same handwriting after all these years."

"Do you really think I give a fuck that I've been caught?"

"I hope you do. Attempted murder is a lifetime sentence."

"There's always parole."

"Maybe," she accedes. "But you seem to have forgotten who I am, and who my parents are. My dad is already assembling a team of his best lawyers. We will keep you in there for as long as we can, so that even if you're ever granted parole, it'll be when the best years of your life are way behind you."

His face reddens with anger, and his hands curl into fists. "It doesn't matter," he snarls defiantly. "The best years of my life were already behind me, long before I even met you."

"If you're talking about your father, who taught you to be this way, he's not the one to blame." His eyes widen at her words—it's clear that her knowledge of his father has taken him by surprise, but Emma has done her research. She always has. "From the moment you chose to hit me, it was all you."

His features contort in anger, but he doesn't say a word, and she knows that her revelation about his father must've left him more shaken up than he shows.

She stands up to leave—there's nothing else to say, anyway, but he stops her.

"I still remember the way you looked in those pictures," he says, and even though his voice is quieter than before, there's still a hint of mockery. "Won't ever forget them."

She lets out a slow breath, trying not to react to his words. In a flash, she's back in college, crying, begging, staying because of his single threat to ruin her family's reputation.

But the thing about a monster is that, once you escape its clutches, it just becomes the past.

"You can keep those memories," she says, without turning. "They're the only things you have left." She shuts the door behind her, sealing him to his fate.

Chapter 18

"I CAN'T BELIEVE it's finally over."

She smiles at the obvious relief in Dylan's voice and adjusts the strap of her bag further up her shoulder. "I know, I was beginning to get tired of it."

He grins and nudges her. "Not of me, I hope."

It's a playful nudge, almost teasing. Her smile fades a little and she shakes her head. "No, just of the project. And a little bit of your voice during the presentation," she can't help but add.

"How dare you," he mutters, but there's no real malice in his voice. She feels him cast a sideway glance at her as he asks, "So, are you hungry? Want to grab supper together? I'll drive."

Her feet come to a halt. It's a very, very tempting offer. "No," she says quietly, "I don't think I can."

He stares at her for a moment, and it's that soft light of understanding in his eyes that cuts straight to her heart. "Right, I understand," he says, just as softly as she did. He runs a hand through his hair and offers her his usual sunny smile. "See you Monday."

"You too."

He heads down the empty hallway; his footsteps loud in the silence. It's way past evening, and the glow of the lights overhead cast long, lonely shadows across the hall. She watches until he disappears, before she turns on her heels.

She freezes.

"Keith?" His name escapes her lips in a quiet gasp. The tall figure comes out from within the shadows; his footsteps silent like a ghost. She didn't even hear him come up behind her. Instinctively, she falls a step back. "Wh-what're you doing here? I thought you were at a party."

He stares down at her; his eyes heavy and half-lidded. It's a look of indolence that he's mastered so well; a façade of nonchalance. But she's been with him for long enough to recognize the angry glint in his eyes; the corded muscles in his neck tense and jump.

"You should be so lucky," he says in a mild voice. "But I thought it best not to miss this...thing you two have going on."

"I told you, Dylan and I are lab partners. We've been working together on a project—"

"Bullfuckingshit," he hisses. "I've seen the way that asshole looks at you. Don't tell me you haven't noticed how he's always smiling at you, and watches you from halfway across the cafeteria when we're at lunch. There's even a rumour going around that he dumped Flo Aryton for you!"

Her eyes widen. There's that little traitorous voice in the back of her head wondering, did he? But she firmly drowns it out and shakes her head. "Why would you even listen to the rumours?"

"Because it isn't just a rumour, is it?" Keith fires back. "He benched me ever since the start of football season. Coach has the final say, but I know he had something to do with it!"

"You were benched because you're too angry on the field! Everyone knows it. You've been picking fights with the other players for absolutely no reason."

"Too angry? That's just a cover. Do you know what Torres said to me the first time he benched me? He said that I'd be left on the bench for as long as you continued wearing sweaters. Which means that you told him what was going on."

"I didn't."

"Don't fucking lie to me!" His sudden shout has her falling a step back. "You obviously gave him enough hints to piece everything together, because that's what you wanted all along, isn't it? For the knight in shining armour to save you, and you can fuck him in your gratitude!"

"How dare you?" she snaps, pushing him back. He immediately grabs her by the wrist to stop her, his grip growing tiger by the second, but still she presses on. "If I were any other self-respecting person I would've said fuck all and left a long time ago. But I stayed and became the quiet little doormat that you wanted. I stayed for so long that I began to hate myself, but even then, I still stayed because we had a deal. I put up with all of your shit, so how dare you accuse me of cheating?"

"Because you would if you could!" he shouts back and shoves her to the ground. She tries to scramble up, but he's over her in a flash. His hands close around her throat in an iron grip. She begins to gasp, her hands come up to claw at his, but he shoves a knee into her stomach and she keels over.

His eyes gleam and he lets out a dark chuckle. "I know you," he says softly. "Everything you do is an act. You pretend to be some quiet, shy little thing, but I know the tricks you play. I know you dope my drinks hoping I'll get caught. I know you've been following my friends around to see if they'll give me away. I know you're trying to find dirt on me to get the upper-hand. I know you, all too well, and that's why you can never leave me."

Tears blur her vision, and her world grows dark. That familiar blanket of sheer helplessness threatens to drown her. Every time she's stuck in this position, she's reminded of just how much stronger he is. Bigger. Faster. She can't outrun him, can't outsmart him, can't outdo him. But even when she feels like she's dying, she won't beg for her life.

This time, however, she will.

"Let me go," she gasps. "Or you're going to kill me."

He only smiles. "No, I won't. What would be the fun in that—"

And then, suddenly, his weight is off her.

Oxygen fills her lungs once more, and she quickly pulls herself up. She clutches her chest, willing herself to breathe. As her vision clears, she slowly becomes aware of the shouting in the background. She looks up, still dizzy as hell, and her eyes widen in shock.

Dylan.

She stares, dazed, as he tackles Keith to the ground. "Emma," Dylan calls sharply. Gone is his good humour; the light in his eyes, replaced by a dark fury that she's never seen before. "Get the fuck out of here!"

The words are barely out of his mouth when Keith shoves him off. Dylan is swifter, quicker on his feet. For a moment, it seems like he has the upperhand as he throws punch after punch at Keith. But the latter quickly recovers and throws him against the lockers. A brutal punch to the gut makes Dylan buckle over, and her shock gives way to desperation.

"Stop it!" she screams, stumbling to her feet. A sharp ache rips through her—Keith must've broken a rib or two in their fight earlier, but she shoves her pain aside and grabs his arm. "Stop it, you'll kill him!"

Keith spins around and backhands her. Fresh blood explodes in her mouth, but she barely registers it as he twists her arm behind her back. A muffled cry escapes her and she struggles against his grip. It's over in a flash as Dylan drags Keith away from her, and she watches helplessly as Keith readies another punch.

"Security! Stop what you're doing and stay where you are!"

Relief sweeps through her as two men in white campus uniforms come running down the hallway. Dylan immediately pushes Keith away and rushes towards her. Through blurred vision, she catches a glimpse of his worry as he frames her face between shaking hands.

"Emma," he breathes, "are you okay?"

But before she can respond, Keith yanks him up by the collar of his shirt. "You asshole," Keith snarls, as he throws a glance down the hallway where, behind the campus security, are several more people in blue. "You called the cops?"

Dylan shoves him off. "I didn't. But you deserve to rot in jail."

"You—"

"He didn't," Emma says quietly. They both turn to her, and she reaches into her pocket. She pulls out her phone and turns the screen to them. The voice app is still open. And it's still recording. "I did."

A look of dawning horror flashes across Keith's face. He scrambles back, only to stop short when one of the policemen places a hand on his shoulder. As the police lock handcuffs around his wrists, Keith throws Emma a deadly glare over his shoulder.

"You bitch," he hisses, the cruel promise of revenge in his voice, "You'll regret this."

Chapter 19

"**C**ONGRATULATIONS."

At the sound of the unfamiliar voice, she quickly looks up. The boy who's striding towards her is tall and lean, with sandy brown curls that remind her of summer. She recognizes him almost immediately. Barely an hour ago, he was up at the podium giving his speech at their graduation ceremony. He'd looked all neat and dapper then, with his hair slicked back and his tie in a perfect knot.

Now, though, his curls are falling into his eyes. Both his tie and jacket are gone, and his shirtsleeves rolled up to his elbows. She starts to look over her shoulder—he's probably talking to someone else behind her anyway, but he comes to a stop in front of her.

His bright eyes are fixed on her face; a small, relaxed grin playing on his lips.

"You're the valedictorian, right?" he asks. When she nods, his smile widens. "That's impressive. I hear you got an even higher SAT score than I did."

"Only because that's all I'm focused on. I hear you're really good at football too. That's just as impressive."

He laughs and rakes a hand through his hair. (later, she'll come to realize it's what he does whenever he's self-conscious.) "Not really, I just think it's fun. So where're you headed, school-wise? I'm sure you have many offers."

"Riverton, actually." His eyebrows go up at that, and she hastens to explain, "I do have offers, but I have a boyfriend. He wants to go to Riverton, and I—well, I don't really want to be away from him."

He stares at her for a moment, and the corner of his lips lift a little. But it's not quite a smile, he looks pleased by her words and also not, and she doesn't quite understand it. (not yet. later, she will.)

"Your boyfriend's really lucky to have someone as loyal as you," he muses. "Look, I know my opinion isn't worth much, but based on your grades alone, you have a lot of potential. So if life gives you opportunities to go places and become something, don't let anyone tie you down, okay?"

She blinks. That is unexpected. She's not too sure what to make of that, from someone who barely knows her at all, so she just shrugs. "Maybe he's not tying me down," she says lightly. "Maybe I'm stringing him along."

He laughs at that and nods. "Alright, you have a point. It's your decision anyway, and I respect that. Anyway, from last year's valedictorian to this year's—congratulations." He hands her the bouquet of flowers that he's been holding, along with a sealed white envelope. "That's a gift card from us alumni."

Yellow daisies. How strange that the first flowers she has ever received are from a boy who's almost a total stranger, and for a completely non-romantic reason. "Thank you."

"No problem." He shoots her a grin and turns to go, but not before calling over his shoulder, "See you around school."

Epilogue

HE ONCE TOLD her that, in order for something else—something better—to come her way, she needed to let the past go. Back then, the past had been Keith, and he had been the better choice that came along.

But now, she's not sure what the 'something better' is.

The future is a blank canvas, and she might have the paint, but she's not sure what to put on it. They've planned their lives together for such a long time that, without him, she feels a little lost. Directionless. She tells herself that she can find a way on her own, that she'll be her own compass, but something still feels missing.

Stifling a sigh, she picks up her pace towards the coffeeshop at the end of the street. It's getting warmer now, the sunlight hits her face as soon as she's out in the open air, and a prickle of heat runs down her spine. She starts to cross the road, then stops.

It's him.

Her eyes widen, and she almost drops her cup. For a second or two, she can only blink at Dylan in sheer surprise. He's standing right there on the sidewalk, with a jacket in one hand, and looking directly at her. When she locks eyes with him, he breaks into a small smile. It's not the wide, sunny one she remembers, but it's there, and it's him.

Clutching her cup tightly, she dashes across the road with only six seconds to spare, just before the light turns red. When she hits the pavement, she comes to a halt. Her heart is in her throat; she doesn't know what to say.

He says it first anyway. "Hi."

"Hi," she says, catching her breath. "What—what're you doing here?"

He doesn't respond to her question. Instead, he stares up at the huge building she's just come out of. His eyes widen, and he looks a little impressed. "That's where you work?"

"That's my parents' business. I've no intention of taking over the company, but since I'm on sabbatical from my old job, I'm doing some research here to help them."

"So you didn't use to work here?" He frowns when she shakes her head. "Why not? You'd be closer to your parents this way."

"Because you were thousands of miles away. And I wanted to come home."

His gaze warms as he stares at her, and she's suddenly very aware that this isn't Dylan with his memories. He's still the same person, but he also isn't. It's like looking into the eyes of a familiar stranger, and everything about this is both old and new.

Her cheeks heat and she looks away, feeling very much like the first time they started dating. "So how did you find me?"

"Your friend Scout. My family knew where you were, but not your exact address. She was the one who told me after she dropped off a pot of daisies from you—which I'm guessing is also important?"

"Only if you want it to be."

"I do, actually," he says, unexpectedly. Her eyes flicker up to meet his in surprise. It seems that, amnesiac or not, he's still as honest as ever. "That's what I've been trying to tell you ever since I removed my wrist brace, but then you left without saying goodbye. Was it because of Flo?"

"No, it's—"

"Because if it's her, she already told me the truth. After you talked to her, she apologised to me and asked for a switch of rooms. She also wants me to tell you that she's really sorry for the hurt she caused you."

Emma nods in quiet understanding. As horrible as Flo's actions were, she's often willing to give the other woman the benefit of the doubt because, after all, she was Dylan's first. And someone who Dylan once loved couldn't be all that bad, could she? "It's not Flo," she assures him. "I moved on because I didn't want to fight with Flo, but I didn't leave because of her."

"Then, why?"

She hesitates for a moment, before she gives in with a sigh. "It's not your ex, it's mine. You got hurt because of me."

He stares at her like she's speaking a foreign language. "No, I got hurt because of him. We were both at the trial—he's the one responsible for the accident. Just because he's your ex doesn't mean that you have to take responsibility for his actions."

"It is because of me. You might not remember this, but I was the one who sent him to jail a long time ago, and he's never forgiven me for it. That letter was meant for me—he hurt you to hurt me. I just—I feel really apologetic towards you and your family, and I didn't know how to face you all. I left because I didn't want to hurt you again."

He frowns. "That's the dumbest thing I've ever heard. I thought you were supposed to be smart. That's what everyone tells me."

Her jaw drops in indignation. "I—I am smart!"

"Not when it comes to relationships, clearly," he points out, and she falls silent because it's kind of true. Even in their relationship, she's always looked to him for guidance. "Look, we all know what that note means. Morgan told me about your past with Keith, and I put the rest together on my own. Mom and Dad aren't upset at all—if anything, they're really grateful to you and your dad's team of lawyers for putting Keith back behind bars. He can't hurt me anymore," he says, before adding, in a quieter voice, "But you did, when you left."

Her eyes widen. "I didn't mean to. I didn't want to upset you again after that whole thing with Keith, and I was just giving you some space—"

"Fuck space," he says bluntly, and she blinks. He flushes, looking a little embarrassed by his sudden outburst, but continues softly, "I know that, when I woke up, it was what I wanted from you. I was hostile and rude and downright suspicious, and you really obliged and gave me all the space I wanted. But I don't want that anymore. I just want you."

She stares at him, barely able to believe her ears. When she doesn't say anything, he takes yet another step forward, never once looking away from her.

"I want you to help me remember," he says. "And even if I can't, I want you to tell me what I've forgotten, what I've missed out on. I want you to help me create new memories, and I swear I won't forget them this time round. But, more than anything, I just want you."

She studies him for a moment. This is no fairytale ending. It's not like he miraculously remembers her and everything has fallen into place. But this is all she's ever hoped for since he woke up: that she would be his choice.

And it seems that, at last, she is.

Her lips twitch into a small smile. "Do you just want me because you have no one else?" she wonders, "Or do you want me because my name is on your wrist?"

"Neither," he says honestly. "I want you because of this." He drops his jacket by their feet, frames her face between his palms and tips her face up so that her gaze meets his. There's a beat, her heart flutters, her stomach swoops. Once again, she's struck by the feeling that she's looking right at a familiar stranger.

And getting to know him all over again.

"Back in the hospital," he says, his thumb brushing her cheek, "when I really looked at you the first time, I felt this: like I've known you all my life, and then never before. So teach me," he murmurs, in a low voice. "Teach me how to fall in love with you again."

She smiles, warm and light and full of hope, and nods.

His lips twitch into an answering smile, just as bright as hers, and he lowers his head to kiss her. Slow and nervous at first, like he's never done this before, and then, when she wraps her arms around his neck, with growing confidence. He tastes of coffee and cake, and there's a new scar on the back of his head when she runs her fingers through his hair. A spark of heat rises between them, and whether it's because of familiarity, or the warm summer air, she can't tell. She doesn't care.

She kisses him back, knowing, all the while, that her world has shifted back on its axis once again.

And keeps spinning.